Alphonse A. Roux

The Artist and the Nobleman

Alphonse A. Roux

The Artist and the Nobleman

ISBN/EAN: 9783337779795

Printed in Europe, USA, Canada, Australia, Japan

Cover: Foto ©Andreas Hilbeck / pixelio.de

More available books at **www.hansebooks.com**

PRICE ONE DOLLAR.

The Artist and the Nobleman,

A PLAY IN FOUR ACTS,

BY

ALPHONSE A. ROUX,

Author of "Louise Necker," a *Comedy*—"Love and Revenge,"
a *Drama*—"Major Peacock," a *Farce*, &c., &c.

Entered according to Act of Congress, in the year 1863, by ALPHONSE A. ROUX,
in the Clerk's Office of the District Court of the United States
for the Southern District of New York.

NEW YORK:
SAMUEL FRENCH,
No. 122 NASSAU STREET.
1863.

THE ARTIST AND THE NOBLEMAN.

ACT I.

Carravaggio's Studio—a large room; a projecting closet in the middle, a window and door at left, a door at right; paintings, chairs, &c.

(A knock at the door is heard.)

Daverna. [*Entering.*] No answer, so there is no indiscretion. [*Enters and closes the door behind him.*] At last I am in the sanctuary that has so long been closed to me! It is true that I have more than once caused Carravaggio to regret saying that I was no judge of paintings; my satires have been most successful; still I admire the works of the worthy successor of divine Raphael. [*Admiring the paintings.*] What a number of master pieces—and unfinished! The very canvass breathes beneath his brush.

Enter STEFANO, *mournfully.*

Stefano. [*Without seeing* DAVERNA.] They refuse to give us credit any more! It is a pity! The confectioner's cakes looked very inviting! How hard, at my age, to have to eat dry bread for breakfast. What! a man here! My brother forbade me to let any one enter this room excepting his fair unknown.

Daverna. Why! it is little Stefano!

Stefano. You here, Signor Daverna!—Who allowed you to enter?

Daverna. I knocked, received no answer and walked in.

Stefano. Depart, signor, depart; go elsewhere to insult with your infamous satires my brother's genius——

Daverna. Come, silence, little embryo, just from the cradle.

Stefano. You—a man—should blush at receiving lessons from a child. Your conduct towards my brother is unworthy of an honest man.

Daverna. Take care, beardless boy!

Stefano. [*Ironically.*] Oh! you need not look so fierce. You do not frighten me.

Daverna. [*Smiling.*] I do not wish to frighten you. I know you are brave for your age.

Stefano. I will prove it in a few years, when I shall be able to handle a sword; in the meanwhile, depart, you, who never cease pursuing my brother with your bitter and unjust criticisms; you, who dare to write that Carravaggio is but a miserable daub!

Daverna. Yes, I say so to wound to the quick your brother's pride, for he feared not to wound mine, but I secretly render justice to him.

Stefano. Leave, insolent and vile scribbler, for I cannot control my anger!

Daverna. Stefano, your youth and your love for your brother may excuse your insults, but repeat to him that his pride will make him lose even to his last friend. Adieu!

[*Exit* DAVERNA.

Stefano. [*Alone.*] They accuse my brother of pride because he will not stoop to flatter the powerful and wealthy. [*A flourish of trumpets heard.*] What means this? [*Goes to the window.*] It is the Grand Duke's herald.

(*Herald heard outside.*)

"In the name of his Highness the Grand Duke of Milan, the "exhibition of paintings and statues will close to-morrow. The "names of those who bear off the prize will be proclaimed to the "people, and the victors will be conducted in triumph to the grand "hall of the Palace, where his Highness the Grand Duke will "crown them and inscribe their names on the Golden·Book of the "Nobility of Milan."

People. [*Outside.*] Bravo! Bravo!

(*Flourish of trumpets—cries, bravo! bravo!*)

Enter CARRAVAGGIO.

Carravaggio. I heard a voice that was unknown to me. Who was here?

Stefano. [*Aside.*] I fear lest I should anger him by saying it was his detractor. [*Aloud.*] The stranger who just left was a foreign amateur.

Carravaggio. Has he discovered——?

Stefano. What?

Carravaggio. [*Going to the closet and feeling lock; aside, joyfully.*] No! no! [*Comes down in front.*] Were you absent when he came?

Stefano. I had gone to buy our breakfast.

Carravaggio. I am not hungry.

Stefano. [*Aside.*] That's fortunate for him, but not for me.

Carravaggio. Had you been here you would not have allowed him to awake me.

Stefano. Then go to sleep again. [STEFANO *takes a chair, sits down beside his brother, whose head he lays on his shoulder.*]

Carravaggio. I am no longer sleepy.

Stefano. Yet you worked all night. Brother, husband your strength, I beseech you, for your sake as well as for mine. What would become of me if you were taken ill? Your enemies accuse you of spending your days in idleness and your nights in debauch. Can they not see your pale and careworn brow, the result of your midnight labors? Ah! had you not forbidden me to speak——

Carravaggio. [*Embracing him tenderly.*] Oh! you are my guardian angel!

Stefano. [*Accentuating.*] So you say, because I love you. This is what I should tell your calumniators: Do you not know that my beloved brother, since his return to Milan, has gained more than a hundred ducats by carving, in secret, little statuettes, that I am obliged to sell for quarter their value to old Solomon Dorcas, the antiquarian?

Carravaggio. Fortunately he keeps my secret! No one thinks I am the sculptor of these statuettes.

Stefano. No one—you are known as a painter, but not as a sculptor, and I, I, your brother, the natural confidant of your thoughts, I myself do not know what that closet contains. A statue, I suppose, for I saw some costly marble brought in, but as yet you have not touched a chisel in my presence; you work by night, and lock the doors, like an alchemist distilling poisons. I do not reproach you with it—but come, candidly, what is that statue—is it copied from your picture of St. Cecilia, that is such a likeness to the fair unknown? Would you join the glory of a great sculptor to that of a great painter? God only knows what hopes I had based on this idea. Alas! to-morrow the exhibition will be closed, and perhaps your statue is yet unfinished.

Carravaggio. [*Who has taken a statuette from a drawer.*] Child! why such wild hopes? [*Embraces him.*] Go to Solomon Dorcas and offer him this statuette.

Stefano. What! is this the result of your midnight labors? Faith, I was unwilling to say so, but it appears to me that for some time past sculpture has made you forget painting. Never mind! thanks to your work, we will be wealthy for two weeks!

Carravaggio. With economy.

Stefano. If you find fault with your steward, you need only discharge him! [*Looking at the statuette.*] A statuette of St. Peter! heavens! what pretty little keys—they'll open us the gates of Paradise, I am sure. Oh! if you would but send that statue—[*points to the closet*]—to the exhibition. [*Carravaggio shakes his head.*] You still have no confidence in your talent. It is a great pity. What a chance you'll have missed. But will you not exhibit the picture——

Carravaggio. [*Interrupting him.*] Come, speak not of this, do you hear? Leave me—I wish to be alone.

Stefano. [*Aside.*] Impossible to discover anything. [*Aloud.*] I am off for Solomon's, and will soon return.

Carravaggio. It is useless; keep the money, pay our debts, and visit the exhibition.

Stefano. [*Aside.*] A likely story! I leave my poor brother fasting! he is thin enough already. [*Aloud.*] Come, kiss your little steward. [*Carravaggio kisses him.*] Good bye, brother—good bye.   [*Exit* STEFANO.

CARRAVAGGIO, *alone.*

He, too, speaks of it! Doubtless 'tis a fine chance I lose, but though I am still master of my painting, the statue is no longer mine. To-morrow there will be two happy men in Milan—the two successful candidates who, by unanimous consent, will be proclaimed the Princes of Art. And I, Michael Angelo Carravaggio, am *I* not envious? There are artists whose fate it is to struggle eternally against obscurity and misfortune—perhaps I am one of these! There are madmen, who take for genius their loathing for the humble trade of their fathers—am I one of those madmen?

                    [*Sits down and reflects.*

Enter LEONTIA *and* BEATRIX, *hidden in veils and cloaks.*

Leontia. Angelo!

Carravaggio. You here, Leontia?.

Beatrix. Against my advice, however.

Leontia. Yes, good Beatrix, you came because I wished you to; now keep watch, lest we be interrupted.

                    [*Exit* BEATRIX, *and the door remains half open.*

Carravaggio. What can have happened? A month without seeing you—a century!

Leontia. My uncle, my adoptive father, was ill—I was ever at his bedside—besides, since we last met, I feared my uncle concealed a secret from me—he suspects, perhaps. Oh! were he to know!

Carravaggio. You would be lost, would you not?

Leontia. Alas!

Carravaggio. Then why return hither—why not endeavor to forget so dangerous a love? Oh! while it is still time, separate your destiny from mine. I will return to you, my betrothed, the ring we exchanged in our moments of rapture—leave me, forget me!

Leontia. Have I wounded you, Angelo?

Carravaggio. No, but I have the pride of an artist. It is most painful to me when I see you suffering on account of my love!

Leontia. What have I done that you should shrink thus? I only expressed what I feared, but you are far more cruel to destroy all my hopes.

Carravaggio. Well! I will tell you all, even were you to think me still more cruel. The Grand Duke, your adoptive father, conceals a secret from you; you were right. I will reveal it: he wishes to wed you to the nobleman and artist, Joseph D'Arpinas!

Leontia. Heavens! is it possible!

Carravaggio. It is the talk of all Milan. Ah! I would have guessed it by the hatred I bear him!

Leontia. But this marriage shall not take place. The Grand Duke has the right to refuse my hand to my lover, but he cannot compel me to wed another! Ah! whatever may happen, you or the cloister, I swear it! Our love is pure, I can pray for it without blushing; and when your fame will reach me in my solitude, when I hear your works praised and your name glorified, I shall think proudly: It was I who understood him the first, and I am the first woman he loved.

Carravaggio. Yes, the first and the last! Ah! Leontia, may heaven bless you!—you, the angel who inspires and consoles me. To-day, more than ever, my heart was filled with discouragement and bitterness; at the sight of you, all has changed. I know not what the future has in store for me as an artist, but you love me! Loved by you, Leontia, I cannot but succeed!

Leontia. You will! Where is the St. Cecilia?

Carravaggio. The statue or the painting?

Leontia. The statue.

Carravaggio. Ah! speak not of the copy whilst I kneel to the model! [*Kneels.*]

Leontia. [*Making him rise.*] Will you not send it to the exhibition?

Carravaggio. No, for I made it for myself alone. I desired your portrait, Leontia—something to which I might speak of you, when not beside me—an imperfect likeness, but one that would not leave me! When I commenced my work, the Grand Duke had proclaimed throughout Europe the exhibition; St. Cecilias were dreamed of by every artist. I carved you as St. Cecilia, without other thought, I assure you, but that of possessing your likeness; and, besides, I never forgot that terrace in Venice, where, at night, you sang, accompanying yourself on the harp. I wished to carve in marble the most charming of my recollections—my idol is there, in that closet, as in a sanctuary, nor will it ever be removed! After what took place in Venice, exhibiting your statue would proclaim our love. I, an unknown artist, am admitted to none of those festivals where the great and happy of Milan alone may alone gaze on you unveiled.   It would say to them: She came to my dwelling—and if the Grand Duke——

Leontia. Alas!

Carravaggio. And besides, as there are so many obstacles to our marriage, what would become of me if deprived of her and of you? Oh! do not laugh at my folly! I love that statue, not as an artist loves his work, but as a lover adores his mistress! and now that it is nearly finished, now that it is like flesh and blood, I tremble in its presence as I would in yours!—there is a defect in the arm that holds the lyre, a defect that three blows with a chisel would correct, but I dare not touch it!—it appears to me as if the statue breathed, and as if the blood would flow! Pity me! yesterday, at twilight, I was kneeling to it—I heard divine sounds coming from the lyre—it seemed to step down from its pedestal.

Leontia. [*Smiling.*] So I have a rival?

Carravaggio. No—a sister.

Leontia. [*Going towards the closet.*] Then show me my sister.

Carravaggio. Stay! stay—I speak with enthusiasm, and then I suddenly despair. I doubt not but you will find in it as many imperfections as I imagine there are beauties. I have not quite finished it, so pray do not laugh at me. Hold!—it is not for you to lift the veil—do not place reality so near to fiction, art and life beside fancy!—to examine my statue in your presence, would but discourage me.

Leontia. You mistrust your genius, Angelo, and by the love you bear me, I implore you to show me your statue.

Carravaggio. You wish it—you exact it—I obey. [*Touches a spring, the closet opens, and St. Cecilia is perceived on her pedestal —a pause—Leontia draws the curtain—a pause.*]

Leontia. Oh!

Carravaggio. Well?

Leontia. [*Throwing herself in his arms.*] You must send this statue to the exhibition to-day—at once!

Carravaggio. Leontia, remember that Liza del Giocundo was dishonored when Leonardo da Vinci painted all the Madonnas in her image.

Leontia. [*After having again admired the statue.*] Shame on me, if, by my guilt, this masterpiece remained unknown! It must be seen, you must triumph! even were I to be cursed—even were I to be dishonored!

Carravaggio. A little glory in exchange for your honor? Never! never!

Leontia. But I know not what I say; your love would honor a queen. [*Admires the statue.*] You are right! she breathes—she speaks! Oh! noble Angelo, great artist, I will be worthy of you,

I swear it! I will fear nothing; the Grand Duke has now strength enough to listen to me, I will have strength enough to speak!

Carravaggio. I said, Leontia, that I consented to send my picture to the exhibition, but no profane eye shall criticise the statue; it is mine alone.

Leontia. I will obtain the Grand Duke's permission, and you will not resist my prayers. Adieu, great artist, a double crown will be placed to-morrow on your noble brow! [*Exit, hurriedly; Carravaggio locks the door after her.*]

Carravaggio. [*Alone.*] Ah! it is love's judgment I have just heard!—how different, perhaps, from that of the crowd!—the crowd!—oh! my statue, the other half of my love, gazed on by the crowd! No! never. [*Shuts the closet, hurriedly.*]

(*Knocking at door.*)

[CARRIVAGGIO *opens the door—Enters* STEFANO.

Stefano. Why you were locked in! [*Looks around.*] Why do you lock yourself in when alone?

Carravaggio. [*Angrily.*] Why have you returned so soon? Did I not tell you to go to the exhibition?

Stefano. The doors were not yet open.

Carravaggio. You should have waited.

Stefano. Why scold me! look!—[*Throws a handful of gold on the table.*]—and our debts and breakfast paid! [*Places meals on table.*]

Carravaggio. Gold!

Stefano. Yes, we are rich! Look at the bright new ducats, bearing the Grand Duke's effigy—the Grand Duke is very handsome on gold!—twelve ducats, no less!

Carravaggio. Who gave them to you?

Stefano. Gave? [*Proudly.*] My dear Angelo, your skilful steward sold, for a round sum, St. Peter and those pretty little keys that were to open us the gates of Paradise.

Carravaggio. What! Did that old wretch Solomon——

Stefano. He! draw from his entrails twelve ducats at once!—it is much less of a miracle. This is the whole story: I was carrying your statuette when I met two strangers, a young and an old one; both stopped and examined your work. The old one admired your St. Peter, and the young one criticised and found fault with everything; I would have beaten him, had I dared!

Carravaggio. What did he say?

Stefano. Oh! he was very severe; his companion continually repeated, but, but—at length he gave so many good reasons that the young man was convinced and asked the artist's name. I told him it was a secret; he gave me his purse, which I took, without counting the contents, for I saw the glitter of gold!

Carravaggio. That trifle was not worth twelve ducats.

2

Stefano. Should I have refused them? Not I! I'm too smart for that!

Carravaggio. [*Smiling.*] The success of this statuette is perhaps a good omen——

Stefano. [*Slyly.*] For that of St. Cecilia?

Carravaggio. How do you know I carved a St. Cecilia!

Stefano. [*Winking.*] Oh! I guessed it! So you would exhibit a statue *and* a painting?

Carravaggio. Patience! to-night you shall know all; in the meantime, I'll give my painting the finishing touch! [*Exit by right.*

STEFANO, alone.

"Patience!" I'm to know all to-night! It appears my brother is more ambitious than I thought!—to exhibit a statue and a painting! the deuce!—no one ever heard of such a thing! So that closet contains a St. Cecilia! But why did he carve it so secretly? He was in such a hurry to finish his painting that he forgot all about his breakfast! Well, I am possessed of a better memory! [*Sits down and eats.*] I dropped in at the confectioner's and had only to show him a ducat for him to give me credit again; his cakes are better than usual this morning! [*Knocks at the door.*] A knock! perhaps some parasite, if so, I'll make sure of my brother's mince pies, at all events! [*Covers dinner up.*] Come in! [*Enter Ludgi and some unarmed soldiers.*]

STEFANO, LUDGI, SOLDIERS—afterwards CARRAVAGGIO.

Ludgi. By order of the Grand Duke, where is Michael Angelo Carravaggio?

Stefano. [*Calling.*] Brother! brother!

Carravaggio. What do you wish, signor?

Ludgi. [*Handing him a parchment.*] Read! [*While Carravaggio reads.*] You have a statue ready for the exhibition—the Grand Duke has sent me hither for it.

Carravaggio. A statue!—[*Mournfully.*]—A statue! [*Goes to the closet and finds it locked.*] You are wrong, Signor, it is not a statue, but a painting I intended for the exhibition. Come, I will show it you. [*Goes to right.*]

Ludgi. I am not mistaken; the statue is in that closet. [*Tries to touch the spring,* CARRAVAGGIO *prevents him.*]

Carravaggio. The statue is not intended for the exhibition.

Ludgi. It is a St. Cecilia.

Carravaggio. Perhaps; but I have no account to render to any but myself for my caprices.

Ludgi. But I am responsible to the Grand Duke for the manner in which I discharge my duty, and, I assure you, I will not leave without the statue.

Stefano. [*Aside.*] If I had as much strength as good will, I would make him leave quick enough.

Ludgi. You hesitate? Well, I repeat, I will not leave without your statue.

Carravaggio. [*Ironically.*] Even were it the property of another?

Ludgi. Whatever price you have been offered for it, the Grand Duke will pay you double.

Carravaggio. [*Ironically.*] And my word?

Ludgi. The Pope can release you from it.

Carravaggio. [*Ironically.*] Signor, you are speaking to a poor artist who thinks otherwise of questions of honor.

Ludgi. The Grand Duke will no longer allow masterpieces to leave his states; your statue was carved in Milan, to Milan it shall belong.

Carravaggio. Ah! Signor, I swear by my mother's ashes that shall not be.

Stefano. Brother, I beseech you, do not be so passionate.

Ludgi. Enough. I have hesitated too long; the Grand Duke's wishes are orders—[*Throws down a purse.*]—Here is gold.

Carravaggio. I despise your gold! [*Throws purse out of the window.*]

Ludgi. Never mind! now this statue belongs to the Grand Duke. Soldiers, seize it! [*The soldiers advance.*]

Carravaggio. We shall see! [*Takes a hammer and rushes behind the closet.* STEFANO *follows his example and stands before it.*]

Stefano. Back! [*Waves his hammer.*]

Carravaggio. [*Behind the closet, utters a cry of despair, the breaking of the statue is heard, the door opens and he is seen standing on the remains of it—furious.*]—Strike now, and murder the artist on the remains of his work! [*Ironically.*] There, take it, carry it off! [*Falls fainting in his brother's arms, who lays him on a sofa.*]

Stefano. Brother! brother!

Ludgi. [*Aside.*] I cannot fathom this mystery. [*To soldiers.*] The painting is in the next room, take it and leave by the back door. [*Exeunt soldiers.*] I must send for a physician and report to the Grand Duke. [*Exit following the soldiers.*

Stefano. Angelo! brother—dear brother——

Carravaggio. [*Reviving.*] Leontia!—where am I?—how heavy my head feels! I have slept, no doubt. Ah! what awful dreams! what has happened? I cannot recollect—am I still dreaming?—am I mad?——

Stefano. Brother, what ails you? You look at me so wildly—you terrify me!

Carravaggio. [*Wildly.*] Who are those men?

Stefano. We are alone—it is I, Stefano, your brother.

Carravaggio. No, see those men—there—there—[*In a whisper.*] —hide me; hide me—they have come to arrest me—they are sbiri.

Stefano. Brother!

Carravaggio. [*Changing his tone.*] Leontia! You know—she returned hither—her eyes sparkled, as she looked at me saying, come! come!—and I, wishing to conceal her from all, I took the hammer and then—then—[*Smiling.*]—I killed her!

Stefano. Leontia!

Carravaggio. [*Smiling.*] Yes, Leontia! [*Wildly.*] St. Cecilia! I know not which; but was it not a crime, a great crime? I should have pitied her, should I not? She was so beautiful!

Stefano. Angelo!—brother! you are dreaming!

Carravaggio. Yes, weep! weep! My fury has respected none but my Stefano. [*Presses him convulsively in his arms.*] May Providence judge betwixt us! Death to the murderer! Death to the sacrilegious wretch! Strike down the lover who killed his mistress! Strike down the father who took his child's life! [*Falls back exhausted.*]

Enter PERGOLA, LEONTIA *and* BEATRICE.

Leontia. Angelo! good news! I have seen the Grand Duke, and told him all—[*Seeing him faint.*]—What do I see——!

Pergola. Stefano, what ails your brother?

Stefano. Look! [*Points to the broken statue.*]

Leontia. Oh! I understand! [*Aside.*] Poor Angelo! I shall never have love enough to compensate for his sacrifice. [*Wishes to draw near him.*]

Beatrice. I beseech you, Signora, allow me to watch over Signor Carravaggio.

Pergola. I see a broken statue, but I cannot understand——

Stefano. My brother has fainted, for he thinks he has killed Signora Leontia, when he broke the statue.

Leontia. Alas! am I cause of his misfortune? What shall I do? [*Clasping her hands.*] O heaven, inspire me!—a sublime inspiration!—conceal those fragments, replace the pedestal! Come, Beatrice. [*Both go behind the closet.*]

Stefano. I cannot understand——

Pergola. But I can——

Carravaggio. [*Dreaming.*] Leontia—dead—St. Cecilia—dead— both—both dead! [PERGOLA *hides the fragments and* STEFANO *runs to his brother.*]

Stefano. I understand now.

Pergola. [*Hiding the fragments.*] By the Cross of Malta, I think we'll do a miracle!

Stefano. Brother, brother, Leontia still lives, the statue is not broken.

Carravaggio. [*Starting.*] Leontia still lives!—and St. Cecilia? Who said she was not dead—— ?

Stefano. I, your beloved brother, your Stefano.

Carravaggio. You! It is false, false! I killed her!

Pergola. What! do you doubt my word, I, Angelo Della Pergola, Knight of the Order of Malta!

Carravaggio. [*Drawing his hand over his brow as if to remember.*] Pergola! Angelo Della Pergola! my friend!

Pergola. Himself, in person.

Carravaggio. [*Drawing his hand over his brow.*] Yes—my friend Pergola—*his* words are not false——

Pergola. [*Aside.*] They should not be!

Carravaggio. [*To* PERGOLA.] Friend, your arm, lead me to St. Cecilia—yonder—no, there. [*Points to closet.*]

Pergola. With pleasure; but you must promise me to be calm and master your emotion.

Carravaggio. Yes, yes, I will try. [*They approach the closet.*]

Stefano. [*Opens it.*] Brother, behold your statue! [LEONTIA *dressed as St. Cecilia is seen behind a gauze.*]

Carravaggio. [*Leaning on* PERGOLA *and* STEFANO.] Yes, it is she! How beautiful she looks! What a masterpiece I fancied I had destroyed! Let me look at her nearer—she breathes—she speaks! Oh! conceal her! quick!—the Grand Duke would purchase and compel me to sell it—he would seize, and I will keep it for myself alone! Oh! shut the door, for I am jealous of my work. [*Falls back almost fainting.* [PERGOLA *and* STEFANO *lay him on the sofa.*]

Pergola. [*Aside.*] The miracle commences.

Carravaggio. [*In delirium.*] Leontia—then was it you I killed?

Pergola. [*Aside.*] The miracle is not yet done!

Carravaggio. Yes, yes, it was her!

Pergola. No, for you will soon see her once more.

Carravaggio. Can it be—— ?

Pergola. I am a Knight of the Order of Malta.

Stefano. [*Throwing himself in* CARRAVAGGIO'S *arms.*] Brother, brother!

Carravaggio. Stefano, my Stefano! [*Embraces him wildly.*] But where is Leontia?

Leontia. Here I am, my Angelo! [*Falls at his feet.*]

Carravaggio. St. Cecilia—— !

Leontia. Do you not know your Leontia?

Carravaggio. Leontia—in my arms—Leontia, my love! Oh! it is you! But where is St. Cecilia?

Leontia. [*Points to closet.*] She is there.

Carravaggio. Oh! yes, yes, I saw her. [*Pressing her in his arms.*] Oh! my Leontia! my guardian angel!

Pergola. The miracle is done! [*Tableau.*

3   (*Curtain falls.*)

ACT II.

A hall in the Grand Duke's palace.

Enter LUDGI, *preceded by musicians and followed by an escort—
they cross the stage from right to left and go to balcony at
back.*

(*Music.*)

Ludgi. In the name and by order of his Highness, the Grand
Duke of Milan, I hereby announce that the exhibition of paintings
that has taken place in Milan, is now closed. The exhibition of
sculpture is hereby postponed till next year.

People. [*Outside.*] Bravo! Bravo!

Enter SOLDI, BOMBA, *four Judges, and soldiers by the right.*

Soldi. [*Announcing.*] The President and Judges. | *The Presi-
dent and Judges cross from right to left.*|

Ludgi. [*After having stationed sentinels.*] Guards, the Judges
are about to deliberate; no one must enter yonder room. Watch
that the orders of our Sovereign be punctually executed.

Soldi. Yes, Signor Captain.   [*Exit* LUDGI *by the right.*

Enter GORI, GAMBATTI, *and artists.*

Gori. [*To* GAMBATTI.] The Grand Duke's orders are severe.

Gambatti. [*Smiling ironically.*] Of course; there must be some
appearance of justice.

Gori. What? Do you suppose....?

Gambatti. No! I do not suppose. I am certain.

Gori. Nay, you are wrong; the Grand Duke is too loyal..and,
besides, he would not dare be unjust in the eyes of all Europe.

Gambatti. Who knows? He is infatuated with Joseph D'Arpinas, his favorite as well as his....

Gori. Silence! Would you calumniate our Sovereign?

Gambatti. No! I would speak the truth.

Gori. Your admiration for Carravaggio blinds you.

Gambatti. I confess that of all the pictures on exhibition, one
struck me as very far superior.

Gori. His! Yes, I think so too! Carravagio is our master, and
will soon rival the divine Raphael.

Gambatti. And how noble-hearted he is! They say, that yesterday, in a fit of anger, he destroyed the statue the Grand Duke
wished to compel him to give up.

Gori. Doubtless that is the reason the exhibition of statuary has
been postponed. However, though we have lost a masterpiece, we
have still a great artist in our midst.

Gambatti. *He* will never stoop to flatter the powerful! He despises their vices.

Gori. Ah! here he comes. How thoughtful and careworn he looks.

Enter CARRAVAGGIO, *slowly.*

Carravaggio. [*To himself.*] Yes, I should have rendered the face more expressive, more fair, more tender..I know not what feeling held back my brush, that against my will, portrayed unceasingly Leontia's features! But what of it?... My triumph would be certain, were the judges to recognize her!... And where could a worthier model be found?

Gori. You seem uneasy, Signor Carravaggio.

Carravaggio. Ah! excuse me, Signori, I had not seen you.

Gambatti. Like you, we impatiently wait that the victor be proclaimed ... The voice of the people has already named him.

Carravaggio. That voice is not always obeyed.

Gori. But this time, it will be; it has pronounced the name of Carravaggio.

Carravaggio. My dear pupils, your friendship blinds you. So many celebrated artists have sent paintings to the exhibition ....

Gambatti. That it is for you to triumph over them; but in a few hours our uncertainty will be over, for the Judges have just entered the gallery.

Carravaggio. Already?

Gori. They are now deliberating.

Carravaggio. [*Aside.*] Ah! my anguish increases! [*Sits down agitated and reflects.*]

Gori. [*To* GAMBATTI.] I cannot understand his uneasiness.

Gambatti. Is not Joseph D'Arpinas a competitor, and is he not....?

Gori. Hush! we are in the Grand Duke's palace.

Gambatti. True!...But see, Carravaggio is wrapped in thought; he both fears and hopes; our presence is perhaps an inconvenience to him; let us withdraw.

Gori. Yes! [*To the other artists.*] Friends, let us not disturb our master; follow me. [*Exeunt all by right.*

Carravaggio. [*Alone, rises suddenly.*] Why did I not destroy my painting as well as my statue?... Oh! Raphael! divine Raphael! never will I be able to equal your genius! Poets may speak with the pen, but you, divine Raphael, you speak with one touch of your brush!... As I look at my works I am discouraged! and yet I feel something there!...[*Points to his brow.*]... there!...[*Points to his heart.*]

Enter LEONTIA, *veiled.*

Leontia. My presentment did not deceive me; it is he!

Carravaggio. What! Leontia! you here!

Leontia. Dear Angelo, I could not master my impatience; veiled and concealed, I ran hither to learn....

Carravaggio. The Judges still deliberate.

Leontia. I know it! have you heard unfavorable news?

Carravaggio. No; not yet.

Leontia. Why then are you so melancholy?

Carravaggio. Ah! you know too well the cause of my fear ... Joseph D'Arpinas competes for the prize!

Leontia. His painting was hardly noticed; those of your pupils are superior.

Carravaggio. [*bitterly.*] They have not the Grand Duke's protection!

Leontia. Nay..the Grand Duke is just!

Carravaggio. Yes, but they say..Joseph D'Arpinas is nearly related to him—that is, the Grand Duke treats him with the care of a father ... The rumors that are whispered throughout the town will have come to the Judges' ears, and will show them the distance between him, the nobleman and favorite, and me, Michael Angelo Carravaggio, the poor painter who dares love you.

Leontia. Angelo, the Judges are honorable artists; why would they commit an injustice you would blush to think of?

Carravaggio. True, Leontia, artists are noble hearted men. ... Ah! were not your hand the prize, I would despise this trial; a vain desire for glory often demands too many sacrifices!

Leontia. I know it, Angelo, and never will I be able to love you enough to compensate for this sacrifice, and yet, God knows how dear you are to me!

Carravaggio. Angel!

Leontia. Ah! if you fancied the happiness I felt in mingling unknown with the crowd that filled the gallery, I stood admiring your masterpiece, and listened, trembling, to the words of those surrounding me; your name was in every mouth...The nobles pronounced it with respect; the people with pride; artists with veneration; women with envy; and I, sure of possessing your love, hoping, proud, I concealed my tears of joy, and ran to hide myself and be alone with my happiness.

Carravaggio. Oh! how fair on your brow will be the nuptial wreath! What a picture I will paint of Leontia following Carravaggio to the altar; yes, Leontia, your hopes quiet my fears; I will conquer, that I may win your hand...for to lose you ... to see you the wife of another...Oh! Leontia...I scarce dare think of it....

Leontia. Angelo, I love you! What more can I say?

Carravaggio. Oh! my life is in these words.

Leontia. Hark! I hear footsteps, it is Joseph D'Arpinas with his friends. Let us retire that they may not see us together.

Carravaggio. Put down your veil, Signora; I will accompany you. [*Exeunt left.*

Enter JOSEPH, DAVERNA, SPINELLI, *Noblemen, by right, and go towards 2d E. left.*

Joseph. This way, Signori—[*opens a door.*]—This is the exhibition hall.

Soldi. [*On the door.*] No admittance.

Joseph. We are all noblemen.

Soldi. No matter. No admittance ... by order of the Grand Duke. [*He shuts the door.*]

Daverna. It appears the orders are strict.

Spinelli. You know that the Grand Duke is severe on that point.

Joseph. Too severe! There is as much ceremony in awarding a prize for painting as would be used were it necessary to behead an Italian noblemen. It is supremely ridiculous.

Daverna. Come, do not be angry, you are certain to obtain the prize!

Joseph. I hope so ... I fear but one ....

Daverna. Carravaggio?

Joseph. [*Disdainfully.*] Carravaggio! the son of a mason, who earns his miserable livelihood by carving Madonnas? No! not he ... another ... Angelo Della Pergola.

Daverna. The jovial Knight of the Order of Malta? He is not an artist ... merely an amateur.

Joseph. For that very reason I fear him. The friend and protector of Carravaggio; he pleads continually in his favor, and has already exclaimed at the corruption of the Judges, thereby insinuating that it would be unjust to award the prize to any but the plebeian ... Since this morning he is with the Grand Duke.

Daverna. Because his Highness wishes to be in a good humor for the day. Why need you fear his decision, you, his favorite his ....

Spinelli. His son!

Joseph. Silence! That name must not be uttered till the Grand Duke pronounces it himself, if I am the victor.

Leo. [*Entering from R. and announcing.*] Signor ANGELO DELLA PERGOLA. [*Exit.*

Joseph. Pergola! Not a word in his presence.

Enter PERGOLA.

Pergola. Good day, good day, Signori; well, what news this morning? What scandalous adventure took place last night? Whose honor was compromised? Which plebeian murdered? Which nobleman exiled from court?

4

Joseph. 'Tis we, Signor, who should ask you the news.

Pergola. I?... I have not met a soul.

Joseph. Perhaps not, but the Grand Duke's closet, from whence you have just come, contains all the secrets in Milan.

Pergola. What! are you jealous of the favor his Highness granted, by calling to inform me that my manners and behavior displeased him?

Joseph. I would scarce have believed that the Grand Duke summoned you for that purpose; your looks are not those of a courtier whose master has been upbraiding him.

Pergola. Ah! I am *not* a courtier! Whether a favorite or not, always the same, laughing at fortune, too small to be provoked, too great to be insignificant, living at court, but lost in the crowd, and seeing pass by me ambition, without losing my modesty and vileness, without stooping to flatter...the consequence is that this morning I was enabled to prove the Grand Duke that he was wrong... he acknowledged it, and to make amend for his suspicions, he gave me his private usher to announce me throughout the palace.

Joseph. Indeed! I thought that honor was only granted to the highest nobility of the Duchy.

Pergola. Precisely. I am an honorable member of that class.

All. You!

Pergola. Yes! and I am none the prouder for it.

Joseph. And pray, what position do you now occupy?

Pergola. That of Grand Master of Ceremonies.

Joseph. Grand Master of Ceremonies!

Pergola. Yes... fortunately, however, my term of office will soon expire. It began at twelve o'clock and will finish at two... unless, in the meantime, I contrive to be slandered and sent in exile!

Daverna. Nay, Signor, you are jesting.

Pergola. I never was more serious. I am deputed to call on the Victor, lead him in triumph to the Grand Duke, crown him, and have his name proclaimed throughout the Dukedom; so, in all probability, my dear Signor Joseph, I shall be the herald of your fame.

Joseph. I doubt not but you would rather proclaim Carravaggio's.

Pergola. Why?

Joseph. He is your favorite.

Pergola. True, I will not conceal that my best wishes are for his success... Had you but seen him as I have, balancing between glory and love, honor and liberty, breaking a statue, his masterpiece, that they might not violate his right as a man and an artist. ... Had you seen him, his brain wild with genius, and his heart trembling with fear and love; then, only then, would you have known the true artist! But justice comes first... You are a nobleman, Carravaggio is a plebeian, the plebeian should deserve the prize, the nobleman should be awarded it. Were it not so, would it be worth the while of a nobleman to be born?

Joseph. Your bitter sarcasms are ungenerous, Signor Pergola! When I, a nobleman, consented to compete with plebeians, my thirst for glory impelled me, and besides, I thought I honored the exhibition with my name.

Pergola. Indeed, in the name of the artists, I thank you for the honor your lordship conferred on them; but you have not revealed all: there is another and worthier prize, unknown to any but you ....

Joseph. Can you imagine ....?

Pergola. I do not compel you to acknowledge it. Besides, not only is Carravaggio your rival in art, but also in love ... the hand of Leontia ....

Daverna. The Grand Duke's niece!

Spinelli. The pearl of Milan!

Pergola. Do I not know it? I, a bachelor and a connoisseur; I, who have already said to Signor D'Arpinas: Leontia does not love you; she adores Carravaggio; if you are victor, she will marry you by force, but despairing forever. Well, Signori, observe the position in which she is placed: her lover will deserve the prize without obtaining it; he, whom she abhors, will not deserve it, but will be awarded it, and will marry her; if anything else were to happen, things would go as they should, and of course that would be against all the rules of common sense!

Joseph. Signor Pergola, I know not the object of your satires; if to test my patience and courage, may I say that I have proved you my patience, because we were in the Grand Duke's palace, but, if you wish, I can give you elsewhere proofs of my courage!

Pergola. [*Aside.*] What ails him! 'Pon my life, I believe he is angry! I did not think he was capable of it. [*Aloud and rather ironically.*] My dear friend, if I wished to have a duel, I would say, candidly, I feel like cutting your throat! It is a mere caprice, but yet, you would have to indulge me in it ... But such an idea has never entered my brain; on the contrary, your presence in this palace is necessary to me; you are the Grand Duke's favorite, so you are the only one I can ridicule, excepting the Grand Duke himself; but, as he is just and good, that is impossible ... I cannot live without jesting on somebody, so if you were to disappear, there would be something missing! ... I really see but one way by which to silence me!

Joseph. What is it?

Pergola. Offend his Highness and lose your position, in which case, I should attack your successor.

Joseph. [*In a rather affected tone.*] Your amiable wit and satire inspire neither hatred nor anger.

Pergola. Such is my character, ever since the Order of Malta has placed me among the happiest and most free of moitals.

Dareina. You! free! You, a Knight of Malta, submitted to the rules of the Order . . . . !

Pergola. That gives me entire liberty . . . When scarcely old enough to be my own master, my relations made me obey them . . . I wished to be a spendthrift, and was compelled to be miserly ; I would have had a mistress, and received orders to marry where I did not love. Then I joined the Order and swore to remain poor, out of compassion for my creditors ; chaste, to avoid the dangers of matrimony ; obedient, that I might throw off the yoke of my relations; since then, I have borrowed without being compelled to return ; I obey laws but not caprices, and I may love any number of ladies, without binding myself to any . . . Ah! Signori, believe me, if you would be free, follow my example, swear obedience, be Knights of Malta . . . But, if I mistake not, the Grand Duke approaches, and my new position demands that I should be beside him.   [*Exit and returns at once with Grand Duke.*

[*Enter* LEO *announcing*] The Grand Duke!   [*Exit.*

Enter Grand Duke and PERGOLA.

Duke. Heaven guard you, Signori! [*To* PERGOLA.] Signor, bring in our presence the Judges. [*Exit* PERGOLA.] [*Aside to* JOSEPH.] Fear not, justice has, no doubt, pointed you out as the Victor.

Joseph. [*Aside.*] Heaven grant that it be so!

Re-enter PERGOLA *with* BOMBA *and Judges.* PERGOLA *returns beside the Grand Duke, who places himself on a platform at back centre of the stage.*

Duke. Signori, what is the result of your deliberation?

Bomba. Your Highness, among all the masterpieces that the most celebrated painters in Europe have sent to the exhibition, but one has been unanimously named as the superior ; that of Michael Angelo Carravaggio.

All. Carravaggio!

Joseph. [*Aside.*] He has conquered . . . . !

Duke. [*Aside.*] Poor Joseph . . . . !

Pergola. Justice is done, your Highness!

Duke. You have my orders ; Signori, follow Signor Pergola, Grand Master of Ceremonies. I desire that my entire Court render homage to the Victor of so many renowned artists. So, Signori, go. [*In a whisper.*] Joseph, stay . . . .

[*All but* JOSEPH *bow and exeunt.*

Joseph. [*After a moment's pause.*] Has your Highness any orders to give me?

Duke. No, not orders, but words of consolation and hope.

Joseph. Hope! There is none for me... Unable to obtain the prize, even with your protection, I am undone. See, the mob rushes to Carravaggio, whose only talent is in producing striking effects, and these seduce the vulgar. The Judges themselves fell into the snare; and then, what Judges did you choose!

Duke. The only competent to be found ... Artists.

Joseph. The only partial: followers, pupils of Carravaggio. You should have named to that office Noblemen; they would not have awarded the prize to the son of a mason.

Duke. Joseph, you know the love I bear you, but my affection is not blind enough to stifle within me the voice of justice. Once, I hoped, as much as yourself, that you would be borne in triumph by the Court and people to my palace, that there I might say, in the eyes of Europe: I adopt the Victor for my son; I will overwhelm with honors and wealth the conqueror of numberless renowned Artists ... Oh! pity me, Joseph, it would have been so joyful had I been able to call you my son and give you Leontia's hand.

Joseph. And I, am I not to be pitied?

Duke. You have at least a glorious future before you, the career of a soldier is open.

Joseph. Yes ... yes, you are right.

Duke. More than once have I desired to send you to my camps; you said you preferred staying by my side; let that wish no longer detain you. Go, combat the enemies of Italy, win for yourself a name, and then I will give you mine. You see all is not lost!

Joseph. No, but the misery caused by my present defeat, can never be forgotten. I love passionately; you yourself approved of my choice, when suddenly that odious Carravaggio appeared and crossed my love, as he now has my glory. He loves Leontia; his triumph insures their marriage. To-morrow it will take place, and, to-morrow, what will become of me? Wounded in my pride, despised in my love, and all this misfortune heaped on me by a plebeian!

Duke. Joseph!

Joseph. And, as a final insult, is he not to become a Nobleman, like me! for you promised the victor the title of Count!

Duke. You and Pergola alone knew of it ... And it was to you I destined it.

Joseph. And *he* will be the recipient! [*The people outside:* CARRAVAGGIO! CARRAVAGGIO!] The escort approaches, bearing my rival in triumph. Ah! do not exact that I should be present during the ceremonies.

Duke. You may retire, but I would see you more calm ....

Joseph. More calm! when everything is lost! name, glory, love! Ah! I no longer trust your Highness's protection ... the love

5

you bear me . . . I can put faith but in my misfortune and despair.
. . . Adieu.   [*Exit, right.*

Duke. [*Alone.*] Poor Joseph ! I can understand his grief at the
loss of the woman he loves, for I lost his mother . . . not through
the same cause, for my rank was far above hers ; I was called to
the throne, and elsewhere I could not love ! Alas ! how often have
I wept at the thought of my weakness !! . . . . But here is the escort . . . Now I must remember that the Grand Duke of Milan is
but the protector of the arts, and has power but to reward merit
and talent. [*Goes and sits on platform.*] [*People, outside,*] Bravo !
bravo, Carravaggio. [*Cannon shots.*]

Enter DAVERNA, SPINELLI, PERGOLA, NOBLEMEN, CARRAVAG-
GIO, JUDGES, ARTISTS *and* PEOPLE.

Pergola. Your Highness, I have the honor to present to you the
illustrious Michael Angelo Carravaggio, the Victor of the exhibition.

Duke. Approach, illustrious Carravaggio !

Carravaggio. Your Highness. [*Bows deeply.*]

Duke. Michael Angelo Carravaggio, in the name of Europe, I
hereby proclaim you the greatest of living painters ! [*Places a
golden crown on Carravaggio's head.*]

Carravaggio. Your Highness, I will endeavor from day to day to
prove more worthy of the honor you bestow on me.

Duke. I also promised the Victor another reward, one suited to
his talent and genius, and a greater one I cannot give . . . Michael
Angelo Carravaggio, I will write down your name in the Golden
Book of the Highest Nobility of our States, and gird you with
the sword of a Knight. Carravaggio, the title of Count is yours . . .
behold it ! [*Gives him a paper.*]

All. [*In a half whisper.*] Count !

Daverna. [*Ironically, in a whisper.*] Count ! a plebeian !

Pergola. Yes, a plebeian ! only a man of genius !

Carravaggio. Fear nothing, signori, I know my own value . . .
I refuse . . . . !

Duke. Refuse the title of Count ?

Carravaggio. Certainly ! your Highness, of what use would it be ?

Duke. Nay, it is not useless when deserved ; it will honor you,
and your crest will be painted on the door of your mansion.

Carravaggio. If I but know to paint it better than another, I
care not that it should be mine.

Duke. But, think you of yourself alone ? When your wife, your
children, will demand the title, what will you say then ?

Carravaggio. To my children, I would reply : your name is
Carravaggio. Were they to ask a coronet, I would give them this
. . . [*Points to the crown he has received.*] . . . and they will not
regret that of a Count.

Daverna. What audacity ! A mason's son !

Carravaggio. True, a mason's son, and one who has not forgotten from whence he sprung, but proclaims it, and glories in his origin! .... Signor, you are but a Knight; with little talent, you would gain a Coronet, but I, a mason's son, I must have genius to deserve it. Were the title of Count offered you, you would accept it humbly and bear it haughtily; I, I do more; I refuse, because, without it, I can render my name illustrious. Count Carravaggio! one of these two words is useless, and notwithstanding his Highness's honor, I would not change the last for the first.

Duke. Carravaggio, the little value you attach to one of the first titles in our power to bestow, astonishes and grieves me. The glory of genius may be equal to that of birth, but both taken together, should not be disdained.

Carravaggio. I was born a plebeian, and will die a plebeian. I came not hither to insult the nobility, but to prove that a plebeian artist has also his pride.

Duke. It would be an insult to the nobility were I to insist. These papers, bearing your name, are void. [*He tears them up.*] I am going to inscribe your refusal in the Golden Book; heaven grant that you never regret it!

Carravaggio. Yes, for if ever I did, it would prove that my name itself was of no value.

Duke. I desire that your painting be one of the finest ornaments of my palace. I will send and make a price for it. [CARRAVAGGIO *bows.*] [*People, outside.* Carravaggio! Carrrivaggio!] · The people call you to the balcony. I myself must appear. You do not refuse to follow me?

Carravaggio. Ah! of all the honors your Highness has bestowed on me, in my eyes this is the greatest.

Pergola. Make way for His Highness the Grand Duke, and the Artist Carravaggio. [*All go to back and disappear on balcony.*| |*Cries bravo! bravo! Cannon shots—a pause.*] |*Exeunt all.*

Joseph. [*Entering by right.*] At last they have departed ... The shouts of victory pursue me everywhere; I fled from the palace that I might not witness his triumph; yet, in the streets, in the squares, everywhere, I heard them utter the hateful name of Carravaggio. I see Leontia, her eyes beaming with joy, come hither to congratulate him ...Leontia! to lose in a day her hand and my title as the Grand Duke's son ... To remain a Knight, and see him him a Count, standing above me in rank ... nearer to the Ducal throne ... and can I endure this?... No, never, never! woe, woe, to him!

Re-enter DAVERNA, SPINELLI, *and Noblemen from balcony.*

Daverna. Well, Signor Joseph, do you not run to see the Grand Duke embrace your rival, and he giving his hand to the fair Leontia?

Joseph. She ... Already beside him! ... And, no doubt, he already glorifies in his title of Count?

All. He rejected it.

Joseph. Rejected it!!

Daverna. Yes ... With the pride of a Nobleman ... He acted as if he feared to degrade himself.

Joseph. Rejected it! ... One triumph for me; but that does not suffice, he has insulted me.

Daverna. Certainly; you are fortunate, Signor, in having personal motives of hatred against Carravaggio ... Were I in your place he should pay dearly for the insult he has cast on the Nobility.

Joseph. What would you do?

Daverna. He should not marry Leontia.

Joseph. But how prevent the marriage?

Daverna. Very simply ... By a duel....

All. Yes, yes, a duel!

Daverna. A Nobleman against a plebeian! Has not the latter already lost the game? Do the rabble know how to fight?

Joseph. Yes ... Yes ... Well ... Yes! ... A duel! ... I'll call him out.

Enter PERGOLA.

Pergola. Ah! I breathe at last! Signori, no more Usher to announce me, no more Grand Duke or Judges to escort: two o'clock has struck, I am henceforth nothing.

Joseph. Then everything is over.

Pergola. Thank heaven! The Grand Duke has entered his rooms to prepare for a ride, and there only remains Carravaggio, surrounded by the Artists, who overwhelm him with congratulations and give him an unceremonious greeting, that is well worth the pomp and triumph of the first ... He, modest and calm, blushes at their praise, while Leontia, prouder than he ....

Joseph. What? Is Leontia with him?

Pergola. Certainly; and, in a week, they will be man and wife.

Joseph. In a week!

Pergola. Here they come. See. Signori, see! How beautiful is the triumph of genius! [*To* JOSEPH.] Signor, is it not a charming sight?

Joseph. [*Aside.*] Ah! they insult me even in this palace!

Enter CARRAVAGGIO *and* LEONTIA.

Leontia. You see, Angelo, my presentiment did not deceive me. Let us go and thank the Grand Duke.

Joseph. [*Stepping between them.*] Excuse me, Signora, if I interrupt your conversation, but I must speak at once to Signor Carravaggio.

Carravaggio. To me!... You have chosen an unlucky time Signor ... To-morrow ... If you will....

Joseph. The conversation cannot be deferred.

Pergola. [*Ironically.*] What? Do you wish to bargain for his picture?

Leontia. But, Signor Joseph....

Carravaggio. Come, it is useless to waste, in refusing, the time in which we might listen. [*To* PERGOLA, *pointing to* LEONTIA.] Signor, will you....

Pergola. Certainly; it is my profession. Sigisbæus was of the Order of Malta. [*Takes* LEONTIA's *hand.*]

Leontia. [*In a whisper to* PERGOLA.] I implore you, Signor, let us not leave the room.

Pergola. Fear not. [*Both go to balcony back.*

Carravaggio. I listen, Signor Joseph.

Joseph. You no doubt suspect the motive of our conversation?

Carravaggio. No; on my honor....

Joseph. Then you do not know what are love and hatred; what it is to see the woman I love in the power of the man I abhor? Know you not how bitter is the envy of the Artist joined to the jealousy of the Lover? Ah! you think you will be happy! No; hope it not. To reach the altar, there remains but one step... There you may stumble yet...!

Carravaggio. Signor Joseph, I never quailed before a threat; you must act, not talk. Did you think that your words would make me renounce Leontia?

Joseph. Whatever means I may use to compel you to, if you refuse....

Carravaggio. Not so loud ...We will be overheard.

Joseph. What care I....!

Daverna. [*In a whisper to* JOSEPH.] So, he escapes you! You let him go....!

Carravaggio. Has Signor Joseph anything more to say?

Joseph. Yes ... I had a proposal to make you, but it is useless; you have no sword at your side.

Carravaggio. No; as a useless bauble, I prefer a golden chain.

Joseph. And therefore you refused the sword of Knight that the Grand Duke offered you. What use would it have been to you?

Carravaggio. Signor Joseph, I am very patient; I am master of myself enough to respect the presence of a lady, which you alone forget; but at some later day, and elsewhere, you shall explain your words.

Daverna. [*Aside to* JOSEPH.] Irritate him more and more!

Joseph. Carravaggio, you demand an explanation, and I will give it at once, before all; I have insulted you because I despise you;

and though the glove of a Knight be yet too noble for the face of a plebeian, I throw it at you. [*Throws his glove.*]

Noblemen. Well done! Bravo!

Carravaggio. Wretch! [*Is about to spring on* JOSEPH, *but is held back.*]

Daverna. Stay ... In the Grand Duke's palace .... !

Re-enter LEONTIA *and* PERGOLA.

Carravaggio. In her presence! ... Oh! all your blood will not suffice to wash out that insult! D'Arpinas, I have not the glove of a Knight to throw back, but my arm will give you a reply.

Leontia. [*Coming down.*] Well, Angelo, is your conversation at an end?

Carravaggio. Yes ... for the moment ... My friend, Signor Pergola ... will please make all arrangements ....

Enter SOLDI.

Soldi. [*Announcing.*] His Highness, the Grand Duke. [*Exit.*

Pergola. The Grand Duke! [*To the Noblemen.*] Silence!

Enter GRAND DUKE.

Duke. We are starting for the grand triumphal ride throughout the Corso; Carravaggio will sit on our right. Come, niece, you will accompany us.

Carravaggio. I thank your Highness, and will follow you. [*Aside to* PERGOLA.] Signor, if you are really my friend ....

Pergola. I understand; trust in me.

[*Exeunt* DUKE, LEONTIA, CARRAVAGGIO.

Pergola. Signori, I will be second to my friend Carravaggio. We will meet to-morrow.

Joseph and All. To-morrow!

(*Curtain falls.*)

ACT III.

CARRAVAGGIO'S *Studio—the picture of the exhibition on the right.*

Stefano. [*Alone, lying on a sofa.*] Daylight at last! and my brother not yet returned. Oh! how I suffered as I counted each minute that has elapsed during the long, long night! ... Where can he be? ... In the Ducal palace, or with his friend Pergola? ... He should at least have sent me word; but then, he was no doubt so happy that he forgot his poor Stefano ... I was present at his triumph; the people greeted him with the wildest applause, and I proudly repeated, I, I am his brother ... A few lads wished to carry me in triumph; I was modest enough to avoid this popular ovation. [*Slyly.*] Angelo might have been jealous ... Oh! how happy he must have been, if he felt but half as joyful as myself.

Enter PERGOLA.

Pergola. I am in the greatest uneasiness ....

Stefano. [*Running to him.*] Signor Pergola, where have you left my brother?

Pergola. Your brother! I have not seen him since his triumphal promenade through the Corso. I came hither to inform him of the arrangements I have made.

Stefano. Alas! my brother has not returned, and I have spent the night in waiting for him; but I thought him with you, and was therefore calmer.

Pergola. [*Aside.*] It is strange! And I thought him at home!

Stefano. Oh! if I believe my presentiments, some great misfortune threatens him!

Pergola. Child! why such thoughts? Let us lose no time; run to his favorite pupil, Signor Gambatti, and ask if he has met him. Your brother was to have visited him after the triumphal march. Go!... Go....!

Stefano. You, in the meanwhile, remain here. I will soon return.
[*Exit.*

Pergola. [*Alone.*] Carravaggio has not spent the night at home! ... Where can he be? I know not! I sent his brother to Gambatti, I know not why. Where has he spent the night? After that insult, he could not have left Milan, I am sure....

Enter LEONTIA, *veiled*, BEATRICE, *at back of stage.*

Leontia. You here, Signor Pergola!

Pergola. Yes, Signora.

Leontia. Where is Signor Carravaggio?

Pergola. [*Aside.*] There, the very question I was about to ask!

Leontia. You are silent! Are the rumors I hear true?

Pergola. [*Aside.*] What shall I say? I should not speak false!... I am of the Order of Malta!

Leontia. Well, Signor, why refuse to tell me where Signor Carravaggio now is?

Pergola. For the best of all reasons ... I don't know myself.

Leontia. I do not believe you.

Pergola. [*Aside.*] There! that's answering like a lady to whom I would swear eternal fidelity! [*Aloud.*] I assure you, Signora, that since yesterday morning, Carravaggio has not returned home.

Leontia. Well, he soon will, for he cannot fight without your assistance, you being his second, and I will not let you depart.

Pergola. Ah! Then I am a prisoner! Of a young lady, too! A nice position for a Knight of Malta! So be it; I will wait with you, Signora, till Carravaggio returns; and then, what do you expect of him?

Leontia. He will listen to me!

Pergola. No doubt; but you cannot, must not change his determination.

Leontia. He shall listen to me, I tell you . . . He loves me . . . To endanger his life, would be but to imperil mine . . . *He* would not kill me!

Pergola. [*Aside.*] She is mad, upon my word.

Leontia. You do not answer; you appear not to believe me; but speak; tell me that he will not fight; tell me so, for pity's sake, tell me so, Signor.

Pergola. Signora, though you may doubt my word, I assure you that I know as much of love as yourself. I have made a study of it, in all the civilized and uncivilized parts of the world . . . In France, it is a game of stratagems; in Spain, a religion; in Italy, a Vendetta; in England, a duty; in Germany, a mere matter of sentiment; in Asia and Africa, a commerce; in America, a mixture of all. It appears that in Milan it is delirium and madness! . . . Come, come, Signora, be more reasonable, and listen . . . .

Leontia. No; silence, silence, Signor.

Pergola. Nay, you must listen to me, for I am not about to declare my love. No! I am one of the Order of Malta . . . I confess that Carravaggio is about to fight.

Leontia. I know it, and will prevent this duel.

Pergola. You have said so already; but, in turn, may I tell you that the man who refuses to give satisfaction is either a fool or a coward . . . You must let Carravaggio prove that he is neither.

Leontia. Signor, I have revealed to you my determination—it cannot be shaken; but you can still be of great service to me.

Pergola. With all my heart, Signora.

Leontia. Name the time and place of the duel, and swear on your faith as a Knight of Malta, that you do not speak false; then, I will leave you, and not await Carravaggio.

Pergola. Signora, the conditions were made during my absence . . . I am unable to tell you . . . .

Leontia. Ah! you are, as ever, pitiless! You refuse to lead me to Angelo . . . To name the hour of the duel, that I may pray for him . . . Well, I leave you, you who are insensible to my tears; I leave you, you who can pity no grief; others, kinder men, shall tell me what you conceal. I will go even to D'Arpinas, if it must be so; will track him, will follow him to the field, and you may tell

Carravaggio that it is Leontia's heart that he threatens with his sword.   Adieu, adieu, unworthy Knight!   [*Exit.*

Pergola. [*Alone.*] There! go and marry to have such scenes before the wedding! Were I not a Knight of the Order of Malta, what has just taken place would make me turn one at once!... Poor Leontia! Poor Carravaggio! Where can he be? [*Striking his forehead.*] Were he absent at the hour fixed upon for the duel I might think that D'Arpinas had carried him off last night to prevent the fight... In which case, I would take his place... Hark! I hear steps; it is Carravaggio!... How pale he is!... Could any accident have happened?

Enter CARRAVAGGIO.

Carravaggio. Ah! you here, Signor!

Pergola. I awaited you impatiently.   How fatigued you look!

Carravaggio. Because, since yesterday I have been watching Joseph; now at last I am certain he will not escape me!

Pergola. What say you?   Could he have attempted to leave the city?

Carravaggio. I was unable to have the duel take place this morning; under different pretexts, D'Arpinas' seconds avoided fixing any definite time, and I spent the night under Joseph's windows ... The whole night his rooms were brilliantly lit ... At last, at daybreak, fatigued and exhausted, I boldly entered the mansion, met D'Arpinas, insulted him, and made him promise to meet me here two hours hence.   This time he will come.

Pergola. Let us hope he will keep his word.

Carravaggio. Oh! I did not leave him thus without any guarantee; a score of Noblemen were present when he gave his word, and all engaged themselves not to let him escape.   Of twenty, one will no doubt have as much honor as a mason's son, since it is thus they have named me.

Pergola. I think so too; let us wait; but, I have something painful to tell you, and yet ....

Carravaggio. Ah! speak, friend; no greater misfortune can befall me than to see the sun rise and still have to delay my vengeance.

Pergola. Well, Signora Leontia has just left me.

Carravaggio. Leontia!

Pergola. Yes; and I was compelled to witness her tears and despair in silence.   Frankly, I require a duel to calm me!

Carravaggio. And now, where is she?

Pergola. She said she was going to look for younger and more amiable Noblemen than myself ....

Carravaggio. Then she has learnt all! Ah! good heavens! may she not return!

Pergola. But she will, and soon. Come, take my advice, let us leave to avoid meeting her, for really it hurts my feelings,—I, a Knight of Malta,—think what it would yours, you, who are her betrothed . . . . !

Carravaggio. Yes, yes; let us go to D'Arpinas at once! But stay, I would embrace my brother . . . Perhaps for the last time!

Pergola. I thought you were with Signor Gambatti, and I sent him thither.

Carravaggio. Poor Stefano! I must leave without embracing him, and in two hours he may be twice orphaned! Ah! never mind! Come, come!

Enter LEONTIA.

Pergola. Leontia! I knew it!

Carravaggio. Heavens! Leontia!

Leontia. Where were you going, Signor Carravaggio? Would you avoid my presence?

Carravaggio. Ah! can you imagine . . . . ?

Leontia. I come to ask of you a moment's conversation . . . with Signor Pergola's permission.

Pergola. It appears, Signora, that my presence is not required during that conversation; yet, the confidant of your love . . . Your common friend . . . .

Leontia. [*Interrupting him.*] Will greatly oblige us by not remaining any longer.

Pergola. [*Aside to* CARRAVAGGIO.] You see, she is determined. [*Aloud.*] I obey, Signora, and will leave you with Signor Carravaggio. [*Aside to* CARRAVAGGIO.] I will not go far hence. [*Aloud.*] Adieu, Signora. [*Aside.*] That young lady will end by hating me . . . Fortunately, I am resigned, being a Knight of Malta. [*Exit.*

Carravaggio. [*Aside.*] Heavens! What will she say?

Leontia. Carravaggio, however grateful I may be to Signor Pergola, I desired to be alone with you. It was the will of my heart . . . Have I been wrong?

Carravaggio. My Leontia, is not a meeting between us always delightful to me?

Leontia. Yes, I believe you; Angelo, I wished to be alone with you, that I might speak openly of the happiness in store for us.

Carravaggio. [*Aside.*] The happiness in store for us!

Leontia. And I hastened to announce that, yielding to my prayers, the Grand Duke, my guardian, has consented to advance the day of our marriage; this very afternoon our union will take place.

Carravaggio. This afternoon!

Leontia. My bridal dress is ready . . . Do you not share my joy, my happiness? This afternoon, Angelo, this very afternoon we will be man and wife.

Carravaggio. [*Aside.*] Ah! what shall I reply?

Leontia. What ails you? Your countenance does not betoken happiness, but rather terror! Yes, I read terror in every feature! ... Carravaggio, in the name of our love! ... What ails you ....

Carravaggio. Oh! nothing, nothing! My Leontia, this news was so sudden .... So unexpected .... I thought that in a week ....

Leontia. Seek not to deceive me any longer. I know all ... They have told me everything. Angelo, in an hour you are to fight with D'Arpinas!

Carravaggio. No, no; you have been deceived ....

Leontia. Then, why blush at your having concealed it? Why those tears that roll down your cheeks? Angelo, are you not to fight in an hour? Then, you care not when our wedding takes place! Then, that marriage for which you prayed so ardently has no value in your eyes! Then, you no longer love me .... !

Carravaggio. What, Leontia! I, I! not love you .... !

Leontia. If you do, why this coldness, this silence ... Angelo! ... Ah! for pity's sake, explain, for I know not if the misfortune of seeing your life threatened be greater than the loss of your love.

Carravaggio. Well, yes; at noon I am to fight.

Leontia. Then it is true!

Carravaggio. And now, no happiness is in store for me till I have washed out that insult! ... But, what you just said ... That his Highness had advanced the day of our union, it was to discover my secret, was it not?

Leontia. No, no! It was not a subterfuge! ... In a few hours our relations and friends will lead us to the altar. You would have spurned my prayers, my entreaties, but when you will see before you the priest, when you will see your bride, radiant with happiness and love, ah! then will you fly from her? Oh! speak; tell me that your Leontia's heart has found at last the means of preventing this fatal duel.

Carravaggio. What! Leontia, can it be true that your love invented this cruel stratagem! ... But know you not that this duel ... My honor exacts it! I must fight with Joseph, and you must ever love me! Shame is on my brow! I blushed in presence of the entire Court when D'Arpinas, the coward, insulted me ... I blush in your presence; I blush even when I think of it! And you, you forbid my being revenged! ... Would you not wish me to live? Would you not have me to be your husband?

Leontia. My husband!

Carravaggio. No, you cannot! For how could I offer you a

hand that could not avenge an insult! Give you a name, even the glory of which would not make amends for the lost honor; how could I press your lips, after my brow had been stamped with shame by the glove of a Nobleman. Ah! I would die with anger and shame at your first embrace.

Leontia. Angelo, you love me not!

Carravaggio. Ah! Leontia ... I! not love you! Look, look, I weep ... And over you! ... Over that happiness that was in store for me, and that in an hour I may lose forever!

Leontia. No! ... You must not fight. We will fly from hence, if we must; we will change our name,—have neither family nor country; but we will live for each other, and in my presence only you will not blush.

Carravaggio. And shall I teach my brother cowardice?

Leontia. Your brother will be mine! He will accompany us, and I will tell him that it was I who wished it ... That you made the sacrifice to my love, and that I cherish you a thousand times more for it!

Carravaggio. Leontia, I implore you ... Renounce this project ....!

Leontia. No, no! Do you think that I could live to hear the result of this duel? ... Every minute of expectation would be an eternity of torture! My blood would freeze in my veins, and when you would return to me a Victor, you would find me mad, or a corpse ... Yes, a corpse ... If you must fight, Angelo, kill me ... Oh! for pity's sake, kill me ere you leave ....

Carravaggio. Leontia! ... Leontia! your tears, your prayers ... Oh! leave me, leave me; I will not gaze on you, I cannot listen ... My love might stifle my honor and vengeance! Adieu! ... Adieu ....!

Leontia. [*On her knees.*] Angelo! oh! I implore you, by the love you once bore me ....

Carravaggio. Adieu! ... One word, and you would make me as cowardly as D'Arpinas! ... No, no! I will not be a coward! Never!   [*Exit hurriedly.*

Leontia. [*Alone, still kneeling.*] Oh! I implore you, Angelo, my beloved! [*Raises her head.*] Gone! ... He has left me ... But I will hasten ... My strength fails me. [*Leans on arm-chair.*] He has left me! repulsed me! Ah! Vengeance! what a passion thou art, for thou even hast made him forget my love! ... And now, what shall I do? What will become of me? ... They will change the scene of the duel, lest I should be present! [*Falls on her knees.*] O, Holy Virgin, my patron, inspire me, that I may prevent this duel! ... Oh! thanks! ... Thanks! [*Rises.*] I am inspired! ...
                                    [*Exit hurriedly by left.*

STEFANO *enters mournfully by right.*

Stefano. I have called on Signor Gambatti; he was not at home. I ran all over the town, and have not heard any news from my brother. Alas! what has become of him? [*Weeps.*] But stay, he may have returned during my absence, for Signor Pergola promised to wait my return. [*Goes to a window at left.*]

CARRAVAGGIO *enters by right.*

Carravaggio. I have seen Pergola; he has promised to bring hither Joseph and his seconds.

Stefano. [*Turning.*] Brother! dear brother! [*Throws himself in his arms.*] Oh! how cruel it was in you to cause me all this uneasiness! ... Here you are at last! ... All my grief is forgotten. I only think of embracing you ....!

Carravaggio. Dear Stefano, believe that I suffered as much as you at the uneasiness I caused! [*Aside.*] Oh! may this uneasiness be the last ....!

Stefano. What ails you, Angelo, your countenance betokens a misfortune.

Carravaggio. [*Aside.*] I have said too much!

Stefano. You are silent!

Carravaggio. Because I know I am about to cause you grief.

Stefano. Speak, speak; your silence kills me ... What, no answer? Do you no longer love me?

Carravaggio. I! [*Embracing him convulsively.*]

Stefano. Well, then I must have committed some great fault, that I render you so uneasy, and no doubt you left me alone to punish me; pardon me, brother, I will make amends, and be twice as obedient and loving.

Carravaggio. Your fault! You! the most obedient and loving of brothers. No, you have not acted wrongly; what grieves me is that a momentary separation must take place betwixt us ... You are still too young to understand the cause.

Stefano. Too young! Am I too young to love you and share your troubles?

Carravaggio. The peculiar position in which I am now placed, compels me to entrust you to the care of my friend Gambatti, and you will stay with him till Signor Pergola comes for you.

Stefano. Signor Gambatti was not at home.

Carravaggio. He is now; go to him ....

Stefano. But Angelo, can I know ....

Carravaggio. [*Rather harshly.*] Come, Stefano, will you obey me?

Stefano. Oh! brother, you never spoke to me so harshly before!

Carravaggio. Because I never felt as I do now.

3

Stefano. Well, Angelo, I will obey ...Without even understanding the motive of the sacrifice you exact of me.

Carravaggio. Adieu, Stefano. [*Embraces him.* STEFANO *goes slowly to door at left,* CARRAVAGGIO *follows him with his eyes; having reached the door,* STEFANO *turns, and both, by a spontaneous movement, fall in each other's arms.*]

Stefano. [*Tearing himself away.*] Adieu, Angelo, Adieu!
[*Exit hurriedly.*

Carravaggio. [*Wiping away his tears.*] Gone! at last! It was but time!

PERGOLA, JOSEPH, DAVERNA, SPINELLI, *Noblemen, entering by left.*

Pergola. Come in, come Signori; there is no one present.

Carravaggio. [*Joyfully.*] Ah! at last! Joseph D'Arpinas, twenty-four hours have elapsed since the insult... Twenty-four hours! Do you hear?... And still you live!

Joseph. Our seconds had to change the locality chosen for the duel ... The crowd had already taken possession of it.

Carravaggio. Now, we are amongst ourselves ... These Noblemen have witnessed the outrage, they must also witness the reparation; I'll brook no more delay.

Pergola. Yes; this room is a good scene for a duel; plenty space, fine light, and above all, no danger of being sun-struck.

Carravaggio. [*Taking a sword from* PERGOLA's *hand.*] Are you ready Joseph D'Arpinas?

Daverna. Carravaggio, have you reflected on what you are about to do? You, whose hand never felt the weight of a sword.

Carravaggio. Ah! my sword will be light enough to find its way to your heart.

Daverna. But, do you not fear ....

Carravaggio. What? Who fears, when his honor is to be revenged!... D'Arpinas, draw and defend yourself!

Joseph. Carravaggio, I should have warned you of the danger you ran by a duel with me. But now, I am ready; let us depart.

Carravaggio. Depart!... Not a step!... Here, here! at once! In presence of all!

Joseph. Here!

Carravaggio. Yes! I am weary of the delay! Joseph, draw, or with the hilt of my sword .... [*Threatens him.*]

Joseph. One step more and you are lost. [*They fight.*]

Pergola. Silence, Signori.

Daverna. Some one is coming.

Carravaggio. Well! even in presence of the Grand Duke, will I wash out that insult. [*They fight.*]

The same—Enter LUDGI *and guards.*

Ludgi. In the name of his Highness, I command you to cease fighting, and hand me your swords.

Carravaggio. What do you wish?

Ludgi. To secure the body of Signor D'Arpinas, for having insulted Michael Angelo Carravaggio in the very palace of the Grand Duke.

Joseph. I! Arrested!

Ludgi. Here is the order. [*Reading.*] " I, the Grand Duke of Milan, according to the laws of the Golden Book, forbid all manner of duel between the two adversaries, Joseph D'Arpinas being a Nobleman, and Carravaggio a Plebeian!"

Carravaggio. Good God!

Ludgi. [*Reading.*] " And I hereby command Joseph D'Arpinas to obey these commands, under the penalty of seeing his name erased forever from the book of the Nobility, and his coat of arms shattered by the executioner."—*Signed the Grand Duke.*

Carravaggio. What have I heard!... D'Arpinas, if you are not the most cowardly of men, you will not obey this order.

Joseph. I have sworn on receiving the sword of a Knight, to yield to my sovereign's commands.

Carravaggio. You also swore to wear that sword as a Nobleman should ... And now you dishonor it.

Joseph. My sovereign has spoken, and it is with regret that I must obey.

Carravaggio. Coward! Then you are a coward!

Joseph. [*Ironically.*] Carravaggio, you who refused a title of Count without knowing its value, you think not of what it is to see one's crest shattered by the executioner.

Carravaggio. [*Ironically.*] True! You prefer your crest to your honor! You dare not become a true Nobleman by losing your rank ... Still you know that I must have your life, or you mine.

Ludgi. We have received orders to prevent this duel.

Carravaggio. Ah! how audacious was your master if he thought his power could prevent it. [*To the guards.*] And you, you are too rash to have undertaken such a mission. Know you not that he threw his glove in my face.

Ludgi. Signor D'Arpinas, be pleased to follow me, and you too, Signori; it is the will of our sovereign.

Joseph. I obey. [*Bows.*]

Carravaggio. [*Springing on* JOSEPH.] You shall not!

Ludgi. [*Drawing his sword.*] Make way for the law!... [*The Noblemen stand aside and let* JOSEPH *pass by.*]

Carravaggio. [*Wishing to rush on them.*] Cowards!

Pergola. [*Holding him back.*] Silence! [*In a whisper.*] I will avenge you ... I swear it!

Carravaggio. Well! depart! Leave, cowardly and shameless Joseph D'Arpinas; and you too, Noblemen whom I despise; you, sbiri, whom I pity ... But tremble!... They will not let us fight! Well, I'll murder him!   *[All exeunt but* CARRAVAGGIO.

Carravaggio. [*Alone and furious.*] A dagger, a dagger, for I cannot use my sword ... No, this carbine. [*Takes it down.*] This will be more certain; every day will I watch for him, however long it may be; and when at length I see him, side by side with the Grand Duke, surrounded by a brilliant suit of courtiers, when his heart, closed to honor, will open to love, when on the very steps of the altar he is about to receive the hand of his betrothed, and all Milan looks on him with an eye of envy, then, then, I shall take aim with a firm hand and he shall die! [*Lays down the carbine.*]

Enter GRAND DUKE *and* SOLDI.

Soldi. [*Announcing.*] His Highness, the Grand Duke!
Carravaggio. The Grand Duke!
Duke. Carravaggio, I have learnt with grief what has taken place, and if you respect not my rank, but my age, I implore you to forget that insult ... I need not explain the motive for my presence here ... You know the true one. Were you not to grant my request, they would say that request was caused by vile and personal ambition.... The hand of my beloved Leontia has been promised you; you may confide in my word. [*Smiling.*] We have prepared an agreeable surprise for you.
Carravaggio. Your Highness is too kind ... I know not how to thank you ... But, without losing the respect due your age and rank, I would remind your Highness that I have been shamefully insulted, and ....
Duke. My dear Carravaggio, you attach too much importance to the follies of a young man, who hardly ever knows what he says or does. Besides, I promise to make D'Arpinas apologize in presence of the entire Court.
Carravaggio. But, your Highness, the insult was ....
Duke. [*Interrupting him.*] I implore you, my dear Carravaggio, let us not think of this to-day. [*Smiling.*] You may, however, to-morrow.
Carravaggio. [*Half aside.*] Oh! Leontia!... Leontia!
Duke. [*Smiling.*] Nay, my dear nephew, everything has been determined between my niece and myself ... But, now, to speak of your painting. The place for your masterpiece has been decided upon; it will be hung in the Hall of Honor in my palace ... I do not come hither to offer you its true value; my treasury is near exhausted, and I could only set aside for you ten thousand ducats.
Carravaggio. [*With joy aside.*] Ah! I have not lost all hope of vengeance! [*Aloud.*] Your Highness ... I regret to state that you cannot have my painting for that sum.

Duke. Never have I paid a larger one, yet I am too anxious to possess that masterpiece not to increase the amount.

Carravaggio. Your Highness ... I do not ask for gold; ten thousand ducats would be too much for my painting; I sell it to your Highness on better conditions for you.

Duke. What do you demand in exchange?

Carravaggio. The sword of a Knight.

Duke. What! a title!

Carravaggio. Yes, your Highness; yesterday, your Highness offered me that of a Count, and I proudly rejected it; now, I would embrace your knees for the pettiest title in your power to grant.

Duke. You should have accepted yesterday.

Carravaggio. I knew not then that a Nobleman alone had the right to be a man; I care not for the title, but I claim the rights of a man, and I have the heart and will of one, more than any of your courtiers.

Duke. Carravaggio, your present request afflicts me as deeply as your past refusal ... I cannot grant it.

Carravaggio. You cannot ....!

Duke. Your refusal is inscribed in the Golden Book; I have not power to erase it.

Carravaggio. [*gradually excited.*] It cannot, must not be! Am I not still worthy of the title I deserved yesterday, because a Nobleman insulted me, because your sbiri protected him from my revenge. Grand Duke, for pity's sake a sword, a sword, if it be but for an hour, only an hour, and I'll devote my life to defend you, my heart to love you, my talent to immortalize you ... But for pity's sake ... A sword ... A sword! [*Throwing himself at* GRAND DUKE'S *feet.*]

Duke. I cannot ... I repeat, it is no longer in my power.....

Carravaggio. [*Rising wild with fury.*] Ah! curse on me, curse on you, infamous Noblemen, who know but to insult men of honor, and are then too cowardly to give satisfaction. Curse!... Curse, on you, people who suffer without thirsting for vengeance ... Curse on you, Court of Milan, that would leave the stain of insult on the brow of a man who loyally claims death or vengeance, that it may protect the life of an unworthy Knight!... The name of Joseph D'Arpinas, written on your Golden Book, is a stain of infamy; his crest, amidst yours, dims the brilliancy of them all ... His cowardly presence in your ranks dishonors them!

Duke. Carravaggio! you forget I am your sovereign!

Carravaggio. My sovereign! He exists no more; I have no country! my liege is unjust, my country debased ...I fly from both forever ... I will seek a shelter from the country that has witnessed the insult; from the world, from my own thoughts ... I go,

I abandon with scorn a blighted land in which there are but slaves and courtiers, with neither courage nor honor. [*Music.*]

PERGOLA *and* LEONTIA *enter at back with bridal escort.*

Leontia. [*In her bridal dress, coming down slowly.*] Angelo!... Husband....!

Carravaggio. What do you wish?... Who are you?... Whom seek you here?

Leontia. Ah! my beloved, here are our friends to lead us to the altar.

Carravaggio. No! No more marriage can take place with this debased heart, no more glory can sit on this dishonored brow. [*Seeing his sword on the ground.*] Down with that wretched painting, the useless work of a hand that has not even power enough to be avenged. [*Tears picture with his sword, that breaks.*]

Duke. What have you done! Your painting! your masterpiece!

Carravaggio. I will henceforth dream of but one; that I will paint with blood.

Leontia. Angelo!... Husband!

Carravaggio. You are widowed. [*Points to his broken sword.*] Broken! the plebeian's sword is broken...Yes, courtiers who feared it so much, behold, it is now a dagger! Adieu!

[*Exit hastily.*

(*Tableau.—Curtain falls.*)

ACT IV.

TWO YEARS AFTER THIRD ACT.

A handsome parlor on a level with the gardens.

DAVERNA, JOSEPH, SPINELLI, *and many Lords entering.*

Joseph. Yes, gentlemen, the day I awaited so impatiently has at length arrived. The Grand Duke, my generous protector, has triumphed over all obstacles; to obtain Leontia's consent to this marriage, he employed all his eloquence and authority as Prince and Guardian.

Daverna. Allow us to congratulate you, Signor, and believe in our prayers for your happiness.

Spinelli. We thank you in advance for all the pleasure we expect at these ceremonies.

Joseph. His Highness has given me, with Leontia's hand, these gardens and this palace. My bride has forgotten Carravaggio, of whom she has not heard for the past two years.

Daverna. But, how is it that Leontia could ever have fallen in love with such a miserable daub! [*Aside.*] Ah! Carravaggio has been paid for the few jokes he made on me.

Joseph. Come, gentlemen, see you not the Prince among those young ladies, who are to bear to Leontia the wedding dress and jewels I sent her? Let us not draw his Highness's attention from these important cares ... Come, friends, let us go and make preparations for the *fete*, that its pomp and magnificence may be worthy of us. [*Exeunt left.*

Enter the GRAND DUKE, BEATRICE, *and some young ladies. The* GRAND DUKE *enters by right back, followed by* BEATRICE *carrying a bridal wreath on a velvet cushion, and some young ladies carrying robes and jewels.*

Duke. How is it, Ladies, that you bring back these robes and jewels? Can the Signora .... [*He hesitates.*]

Beatrice. Yes, your Highness, Signora Leontia refused to accept them.

Duke. Impossible!

Beatrice. Alas! your Highness, but too true!

Duke. What shall I do? Good heavens! what shall I do? Ladies await my orders in the next room. [*Aside.*] Poor Leontia! [*Exeunt ladies by back right.*

Duke. [*Alone.*] She refused them! Still she had yielded to my prayers ... Now, I fear that my reproaches will not conquer her obstinacy ... Some one approaches ... Ah! it is Signor Della Pergola ... He no doubt has encouraged Leontia in her refusal, by speaking continually of Carravaggio.

Enter PERGOLA.

Pergola. Your Highness, I come to ask you to grant me a request.

Duke. You, Signor!

Pergola. I astonish your Highness, do I not? ... For the last two years, ever since the departure of my poor friend Carravaggio, I am less inclined than before to solicit your Highness's favors ... I have not even attempted to enliven you as I once did, because ... Because ... Your behavior has not pleased me as much as formerly ... You prevented my keeping a promise, not of love—for I am a Knight of Malta—but of friendship, and I have not forgotten it.

Duke. What! Signor, such language! ... Addressed to me ....

Pergola. I have spoken candidly, as I always did, you know it; and it proves that I would be once more your friend, and that I hope a reconciliation may take place between your Highness and my humble self. [*Bows.*] Yes, your Highness, to-day a *fete* will take place—a marriage at your Highness's Court. I wish to become, but only for twenty-four hours, the same jovial companion I once was, and I request of you that I may be re-instated in my former functions of Grand Master of Ceremonies.

Duke. Pergola, are you speaking seriously, for I always doubt your words ... and the very tone in which you uttered your demand ....

Pergola. I never was more serious, your Highness; more than two years have elapsed in solitude, without robbing my smile, my eyes, my words, of that ironical expression they once wore; but believe me, at this moment I am not jesting. I repeat, your Highness, will you re-instate me as Grand Master of Ceremonies?

Duke. Were you not, a few days since, greatly opposed to this marriage?

Pergola. A few days since, I was, but from yesterday, I have changed my mind.

Duke. No doubt, yielding to your advice, Leontia has just refused to accept the bridal dress that her future husband sent her.

Pergola. Well, thanks to my advice, in a few moments hence, she will accept it.

Duke. What do you say?

Pergola. I will answer for it.

Duke. Signor, do not jest any longer.

Pergola. Your Highness, I assure you that I am serious, though a marriage is in question; and though I am not fond of Signor Joseph, yet I will speak in his behalf, and am sure I will shake Leontia's determination.

Duke. Do that, and I will ever be your friend; and, to begin with, I give you charge of the preparations of ceremonies.

Pergolo. Your Highness, the first thing I must do, is to speak to the Signora.

Duke. She will be here in a moment ... Think of it ... My happiness is in your hands. Adieu, friend. [*Exit back.*

Pergola. [*Alone, drawing forth a letter.*] Well, Angelo, you wish it, and against my will, I must obey. Leontia shall wed Joseph D'Arpinas, and at your express request, I will bring about, and do the honors of this marriage. But, why the deuce was I foolish enough to bind my wild and brilliant destiny to Carravaggio's unlucky star! ... From the day I became his friend, I found that my character had become gloomy and melancholy; I, who thought such a thing impossible till then.... I talked reasonably, I wept at his cruel fate, yes, wept! ... Well, after all, one must do something for one's friends.

Enter Leontia.

Leontia. I have just left his Highness, who told me you wished to speak to me.

Pergola. It is true.

Leontia. I listen.

Pergola. Signora ... [*Aside.*] It is more embarrassing than I thought.

Leontia. Well, Signor?

Pergola. Well!... [*Aside.*] Come, I must have courage; I promised, and am a Knight of Malta. [*Aloud.*] Signora, to-day is fixed upon by his Highness for .... [*Hesitates.*]

Leontia. For a marriage that is hateful to me, and that I reject with all my heart.

Pergola. I am about to surprise you, Signora, but ... But ... I think you are wrong ....

Leontia. Wrong?...What do you say ....?

Pergola. I knew I would surprise you!... I, myself, notwithstanding the resolution I took, feel it difficult to give you such advice; I know you may not take it, and that you will begin by reproaching me and calling me an egotist. Heaven knows that I pity your grief and wish to see you happy; for these reasons I advise you to wed Signor Joseph.

Leontia. He!...You take a cruel pleasure in driving me to despair; you, who, but a few days since advised me to refuse Joseph's hand.

Pergola. A few days since I was sincere, and I am still the same.

Leontia. No, no; you mock my torments, and that to-day, when I need your assistance the most ... Ah! it is wrong, very wrong!

Pergola. Come, you will not believe that I am serious; you are like his Highness, who a few moments since made me repeat twice the same thing, so improbable it appeared to him that I could utter a dozen words in succession without jesting!... It is my destiny to be mistrusted! Yes, Signora, I speak sincerely ...You must never see Carravaggio!

Leontia. Good heavens! never!

Pergola. And for your own happiness you must renounce him.

Leontia. Happiness! happiness! Afar from Carravaggio ... The wife of his enemy! Happiness! after having perjured myself ... I repeat, Signor, you seek to deceive me; you cannot think of what you say...Or rather, you never were Carravaggio's friend.

Pergola. I, not his friend!... Signora, you are too severe!... Ah! I have now the right to say to you ... It is wrong, very wrong!... I, not his friend!... And if I were not, would I speak so strangely...Or rather, would I be as serious as I have been for the past hour?... It is with the greatest struggle, Signora, that I repeat: Carravaggio will never be your husband ... I fulfil a duty, a painful duty, but I must fulfil it.

Leontia. And my promises ....?

Pergola. Ah! true, your promises ... [*Aside.*] I have found a woman ready to keep her word! perhaps the only one! And her lover exempts her from keeping it, too! [*Aloud.*] Here, Signora, read; this letter relieves you from all promises.

Leontia. A letter!

Pergola. Yes; for to convince you of the truth of what I am saying, I must have recourse to this.

Leontia. A letter from Angelo ....?

Pergola. To his friend; for, as you will see, he still believes me his friend.

Leontia. [*Reading.*] "DEAR PERGOLA:— I know what has "taken place in Milan. When you will receive this letter they "will no doubt be prepared to celebrate the marriage, of which I "could not think for some time past without indignation." [*She looks at* PERGOLA.]

Pergola. You see!

Leontia. [*Reading.*] "So, my dear Pergola, think of changing "Leontia's determination ...Tell her that I release her from her "vows ...Now that it is impossible for me to keep my oath." [*She weeps.*]

Pergola. [*Aside.*] Perhaps he wishes to become a Knight of Malta.

Leontia. [*Reading.*] "Tell her I implore her to obey his High- "ness, and accept the husband he destines her. Adieu; I depend "on your friendship.—MICHAEL ANGELO CARRAVAGGIO." [*Hides her head in her hands.*]

Pergola. Written and signed by himself.

Leontia. Well, Signor, behold him whose honor and constancy you ever spoke of!

Pergola. True! ... As regards constancy in love, I will never answer for a friend as long as I live; it is enough to do to be responsible for myself ...When I succeed in so doing ....

Leontia. [*Reading again.*] "Tell her I implore her to obey his "Highness, and accept the husband he destines her." ... Signor, reply to your friend, that I will obey... Not his Highness's command, but his ... He wishes it, I will be his enemy's wife.

Pergola. [*Aside.*] How easily women understand vengeance. [*Aloud.*] Signora, what are your plans?

Leontia. I will yield to Carravaggio's will ... Have I not always obeyed his wishes, his caprices? [*Walking to and fro agitated.*] Where are the Noblemen who are to witness my happiness? ... And the noble Knight whose glorious wife I am to be, where is he now? I await him ... Ah! what means this delay?

Pergola. Signora, be calm ... They are coming.

Leontia. Ah! already! ... Never mind, let them come! ... I will be happy, very happy to receive their congratulations. [*Aside.*] Before to-night I shall be dead! [*Aloud.*] Let them come, the noble lords!

Pergola. Is she serious? [*Aside.*] Come, she is one of her sex, after all, and has made up her mind in a moment.

Enter DUKE, JOSEPH, DAVERNA, SPINELLI, BEATRICE, *Ladies and Nobles.*

Leontia [*Going to* DUKE.] Your Highness, I awaited you. This morning I was guilty; pardon me, I beseech you; I submit to your will. Signor Joseph D'Arpinas, here is my hand.

Joseph. Ah! Signora, I scarce can believe such happiness.

Pergola. [*Aside.*] Nor I; I scarce can believe ... And I don't believe ....

Duke. Leontia, my child ... Ah! now all my wishes are fulfilled, and it is to you I am indebted ....

Leontia. Your Highness! [*Aside.*] Alas! [*In a forced tone.*] I thank you, Signor Joseph, for your generosity; I accept those gifts ... I am happy, proud, to become your wife ... But, permit me to retire for a moment. Come, Beatrice, and you too, Ladies, I need your kind services. [LEONTIA *and Ladies exeunt.*

Pergola. [*Aside.*] Poor Leontia! She is too amiable with Joseph. She must be mad!

Duke. Signor Daverna, I have some orders to give you. [*Speaks in a whisper to* DAVERNA, *who exits.*]

Joseph. [*Kissing the* DUKE'S *hand.*] Your Highness, I know not how to thank you for the kindness you have shown me ....

Duke. By always proving yourself worthy of it. [*Aside to* PERGOLA.] Signor, I would be pleased if you allowed me a chance to give you proofs of my gratitude.

Pergola. [*In a low tone.*] You owe me nothing, your Highness, for I am so sorry at what I have done, that I have scarce courage to perform my duties.

Duke. Come, come, I will assist you if necessary. [*To Nobles.*] Signori, I have named Signor Della Pergola Grand Master of Ceremonies; you will obey him as you would myself. [*All bow—flourish of trumpets in the gardens.*]

Enter LEONTIA *in her bridal dress,* BEATRICE, *Ladies, Heralds, and Musicians at back.*

Duke. [*Going to* LEONTIA.] Leontia, Joseph, before leading you to the altar, I will give both of you a new proof of my kindness and love.

Daverna. [*Entering.*] Your Highness's orders are executed.

Duke. Thanks, Signor Daverna ... Noblemen who surround me, I required your presence to give more brilliancy to the double ceremony about to take place ... Heralds, approach, bring hither the brilliant crest, the glorious coat of arms. [*Heralds obey his orders.*]

Pergola. [*Aside.*] What next, I wonder?

Duke. Joseph ... Signor D'Arpinas, I, Grand Duke of Milan, in the eyes of my Court adopt you as my son.

Joseph. Ah! your Highness!... Father! [*Falls at his knees.*]

Duke. In my arms, Joseph, my son! [*Embraces him.*] This crest is mine; in future it shall be substituted for yours, and you will show yourself worthy of it by always acting as a brave and loyal Knight.

Joseph. I swear it!

Duke. Signor Della Pergola, you know the customs ... It is now your duty to give orders in my stead. [*Takes a seat at back.* PER-GOLA *leads* LEONTIA *to him and makes her sit down with the* GRAND DUKE.

Pergola. Heralds, approach! [*Flourish—he takes* JOSEPH *by the hand and leads him to the middle of the stage.*] Noblemen, you have heard his Highness's commands; it pleases him to adopt this Nobleman as his son, and to allow him the crest of his noble house ... If there be one amongst you who thinks it his duty to object to this, who considers Signor D'Arpinas unworthy of such an honor, let him stand forth and give his reasons.

Daverna. No, no; not one!   ·

Nobles. No, no!

Pergola. [*Aside.*] Ah! were I not Grand Master of Ceremonies! [*Aloud.*] Then, you all approve, without restriction, of his Highness's choice?

Nobles. Yes! all, all!

Enter CARRAVAGGIO.

Carravaggio. All ... But me!.... [*Strikes the crest with his sword and overthrows it.*]

All. Carravaggio! [*General excitement—*LEONTIA *and* PER-GOLA *run to* CARRAVAGGIO *and press him in their arms.*]

Pergola. Is it possible, my friend!

Leontia. Ah! it is you! You!...Who love me still ... Could it be otherwise?

Duke. Carravaggio ... I could not foresee your return ... And your audacity ....

Carravaggio. Your Highness, I have now the right to appear at your Court, to overthrow that crest, and cross swords with that unworthy Nobleman!... See, see these papers; I too am a Knight. [*Gives papers to* DUKE.]

Pergola. Ah, ah! Signor de Carravaggio, it is now my duty to herald you!

Leontia. [*Aside.*] Holy Virgin, my patron Saint, thanks, thanks!

Duke. [*To* JOSEPH, *having looked over the papers.*] Joseph, he is a Nobleman.   ·

Nobles. A Nobleman!

Carravaggio. Yes; I was a Nobleman in heart, and now I am one

in heart and name. [*Bitterly.*] Yes, in name ... And to earn that
title, oh! the labor it cost me! ... The outrages I had to submit to!
... I, once so proud, whose brow had never bent to any, whose
talent never disguised either vice, deformity, or ridicule, I flattered
pride—the vanities of Princes and Noblemen; I painted a tyrant
as Titus, his mistress as Lucretia, and gave the manly features of
the republicans of ancient Rome, to the courtiers of the present
day ... I crawled at the feet of all the sovereigns in Europe ... I
slavishly sold them my talent and my name ... I debased myself
in my own eyes,—[*bitterly.*]—that I might win these titles! ... But
the sovereigns offered me gold, as the Artist's salary, gold, only
gold ... At last the Spaniards entered Italy; I joined the army,
fought a score of battles, and it was on the field of honor, after
having saved an entire town from ruin, that I was knighted.

Duke. I have read these papers, and confess with pleasure, Carravaggio, that you merit our esteem and admiration ... But, why
must you return ....

Carravaggio. Joseph D'Arpinas, you did not expect it, did you?
... The Grand Duke's favorite, the future husband of the fair
Leontia, you were intoxicated with happiness, and I, I savored in
advance all the pleasures of vengeance! ... I would not have had
any one trouble your dreams by mentioning the name of Carravaggio; I would not have had Leontia refuse your hand ... To attack
you when unfortunate, when foiled in your love, was not sufficient
vengeance for me; I waited the moment when all your dreams being
realized, I could appear and say: You are a wretch, a coward!
Your life, I must have your life to wash out my insult! Draw!
behold my witness. [*Points to* PERGOLA.] All these Noblemen
will hasten to be yours. Draw! here, at once, we will fight till
one of us falls.

Joseph. Well, well! ... Yes, till one of us falls.

Duke. [*In a whisper.*] Joseph, remember that you must remove
the stain from that crest, henceforth yours as well as mine.

Joseph. [*To* DUKE, *in low tone.*] Father, I will live worthy of
you, or die.

Pergola. [*During this last dialogue* PERGOLA *has spoken with* DA-
VERNA *and* SPINELLI.] Signori, it has been agreed between the
seconds that the principals will fight immediately, with swords, in
the garden; your Highness, and you, Ladies, I beseech you to
withdraw.

Duke. The Ladies may, but I will remain.

Leontia. And I; do not leave me, good Beatrice. [*Ladies retire
to back, the middle of the stage is cleared.*]

Carravaggio. Come, I await you, Signor Joseph.

Joseph. [*Drawing his sword.*] I am at your disposal, Signor.
[*Both go to garden at back.*]

11

Pergola. Signori, make way for the gentlemen.

Leontia. And may Heaven protect the right! [*She leans on* BEATRICE.—*Music.*—CARRAVAGGIO *and* JOSEPH *cross their swords.* —*A pause.*—*All look at the duel taking place with anxiety.*

Carravaggio. There, wretch, this may be your punishment!

Joseph. And yours!

Leontia. Ah! Angelo! [*Makes a movement.*]

Duke. [*Stopping her.*] Stay, stay, Signora, and let all be silent; a step, a word, might decide the fate of the duel.

Leontia. [*Aside.*] Holy Virgin, protect Angelo!

Duke. See! my son has the advantage!

Leontia. Good heavens!

Duke. He will throw his opponent.

Leontia. Ah! my strength fails me! [BEATRICE *supports her.*]

Duke. Ah! my son is disarmed! [*Hides his head in his hands.*]

Leontia. Oh! Holy Virgin, thanks, thanks!

Joseph. [*Tearing open his coat.*] Strike, and kill me!... I have insulted you.

Carravaggio. Signor Joseph, take your sword and let the fight continue.

Enter STEFANO.

Stefano. [*Entering hurriedly.*] Brother!... Where is he? [*All look towards back, he runs there.*] Angelo! brother!

Carravaggio. Stefano! [*Embraces him.*] Poor child! why come hither?

Stefano. Heavens! What are you doing with that sword?... Fighting!... Do you wish to die, and kill me at the same time!

Pergola. Stefano, stand back!

Stefano. Stand back! Shall I let him kill my brother? My whole happiness is centred in Angelo!... I love but him! live but for him! I ask nothing but my brother. I must have him; he is mine, my only wealth; you shall not tear him from me! [*Drags* CARRAVAGGIO *to the middle of the stage.*]

Joseph. Signor Carravaggio, what am I to do?

Carravaggio. Take up your sword, and let the duel continue; your Highness, command that child to depart.

Duke. Come, child, go!... You must.

Leontia. [*Approaching, in a whisper.*] Stefano, remain, I beseech you!

Stefano. [*Astonished and aside.*] The fair unknown!... No, your Highness; you may drive me away, but I will not willingly leave this spot! [*Recognizing* JOSEPH.] Ah!... I am not mistaken ... It is you whom ....

Joseph. [*Aside.*] Heavens! [*Aloud.*] You are wrong. I do not know you.

Stefano. Ah! but I do.   I recognize you full well.

Joseph. [*In a whisper to* STEFANO.] I implore you, be silent!

Stefano. And why should I?   I am not ungrateful!

Carravaggio. What do you mean, Stefano?

Stefano. [*After having pressed* JOSEPH's *hand.*] Listen, brother: I was swimming the other day in the lake, and came near drowning, when a young Nobleman riding past saw the danger I ran, and dived instantly after me, just as my strength was failing.   He seized me with one hand, and swimming to the shore with the other, lifted me safely on the bank; then he ordered his servants to take care of me and fled to avoid my gratitude.

Duke. Joseph, my son, is it possible?

Joseph. Father ....

Spinelli. Yes, your Highness; I was present and recognize now the boy, but I knew not then that he was Carravaggio's brother.

Duke. Well, Signor Carravaggio, what say you to this?

Carravaggio. Your Highness ....

Stefano. Brother, he saved my life! ....

Carravaggio. He dishonored mine! ....

Duke. Dishonored yours?   A false pride blinds you, Signor Carravaggio ... Besides, will not your conduct prove to all how bright and unsullied your honor? ... I may now disclose to you the deep regret of Signor D'Arpinas ....

Joseph. Your Highness, I confess now, without blushing, that in a fit of vile jealousy, I insulted, as no worthy Knight should, a noble and great Artist.   I regret it most deeply ... Signor Carravaggio, I consent in advance to give you any satisfaction you may demand, and I will not consider my honor retrieved till my fault is wiped out.

Carravaggio. Well, Signor D'Arpinas, the Mussulmen have just attacked the Isle of Rhodes, and ....

Joseph. You have anticipated me, Signor Carravaggio; I will go and deserve my sovereign's favors.   Adieu!

[*Bows and exit.*

Duke. My son!

Leontia. Angelo! my beloved Angelo!

[CARRAVAGGIO *kisses her hand.*

Pergola. [*To Noblemen.*] Now, Signori, you must believe that the mason's son is at least your equal.

.

THE END.

ANY copyright hereafter granted, under the law
the United States, to the author or proprietor of an
dramatic composition, designed or suited for pub
representation, shall be deemed and taken to con.
upon the said author or proprietor, his heirs or assign
along with the sole right to print and publish th
said composition, the sole right also to act, perforn
or represent the same, or cause it to be acted, pei
formed, or represented, on any stage or public plac
during the whole period for which the copyright ²
obtained; and any manager, actor, or other persor
acting, performing, or representing the said composition, without or against the consent of the said author or proprietor, his heirs or assigns, shall be liabl
for damages, to be sued for and recovered by action
on the case, or other equivalent remedy, with costs
of suit, in any court of the United States—such
damages in all cases to be rated and assessed at suc'
sum not less than one hundred dollars for the first,
and fifty dollars for every subsequent performance
as to the court having cognizance thereof shall appear to be just.